For Seth and Aphra
B. M.

For Mara, Liz, Amelia and David
H. C.

First published 1987 by Walker Books Ltd
87 Vauxhall Walk, London SE11 5HJ

This edition published 2011

2 4 6 8 10 9 7 5 3 1

This book has been typeset in Godlike

Printed in China

British Library Cataloguing in Publication Data:
a catalogue record for this book is available from the British Library

ISBN 978-1-4063-2349-8

www.walker.co.uk

# THE YELLOW HOUSE

## BLAKE MORRISON

## ILLUSTRATED BY HELEN CRAIG

WALKER BOOKS
AND SUBSIDIARIES
LONDON · BOSTON · SYDNEY · AUCKLAND

Every day we passed the yellow house

on our way to the park, Mum and

me and my little sister Jenny.

The house was on its own.

It looked old, sad and rather scary.

At the little wooden gate Mum would
lift me up to show me the garden.
There was a lawn, a goldfish pond,
a greenhouse, an apple tree, a dustbin,
a garden gnome. But never any people,
never any children.

One day Jenny dropped her teddy near
the yellow house and Mum went back
to fetch it. I climbed the wooden gate
all by myself. Inside the garden was
a boy in dungarees and a bobble hat.
He waved to me.

"Come inside!" he shouted.
"Come and play with me."

I pulled myself over and slid my legs
down till they touched the pebbly path.
The garden looked huge. The boy stood
on the lawn.

"Come and see this!" he shouted.
"Come and see this."

I ran and looked. In the long grass
a tiger was playing with its cubs.

They cuffed and scratched each other.

They growled at me.

But the boy had moved off

to the goldfish pond.

"Come and see this!" he shouted.

"Come and see this."

I ran and looked. A white dolphin

swam out from the lily pads, leapt in

the air and splashed down on the water.

It wiggled its tail at me.

But the boy had gone inside

the greenhouse.

"Come and see this!" he shouted.

"Come and see this."

I ran and looked. A green snake was
winding its body round the cane of a
tomato plant. It shimmied and hissed.
It stuck out its tongue at me.

But the boy was standing under
the apple tree.
"Come and see this!" he shouted.
"Come and see this."

I ran and looked. A pelican was roosting

on a branch. It swallowed an apple with a

*chomp chomp.* It wobbled its pouch at me.

But the boy had opened the dustbin.

"Come and see this!" he shouted.

"Come and see this."

I ran and looked. Inside the dustbin
a panda was reading a newspaper.
It squinted and ho-hoed.
It lifted its hat when it saw me.

But the boy was striding through
the front door of the house.
"Come and see this!" he shouted.
"Come and see this."

I ran to look but the

boy had closed the door.

I stretched, right up

on my tiptoes, but

the handle was too high

for me. I rang the bell

but no one came to answer.

Now Mum had seen me and was calling

from the wooden gate. She looked cross.

I walked very slowly down the pebbly path.

Mum lifted me back over the gate.

"Where have you been?" she asked.

"Jenny was worried."

Then Mum gave me

a great big kiss.

We still go past the yellow house on our way to the park, Mum and me and my little sister Jenny. Mum lifts me up to see the garden. There is a lawn, a goldfish pond, a greenhouse, an apple tree, a dustbin, a garden gnome. Never any people, though, never any children, never the boy who waved to me. But I know one day he'll be there again, calling me in to play.